Mouse in the Manger

TIM WYNNE-JONES
Illustrated by Elaine Blier

Woodstock Public Library
VIKING

The woodpile is not a good home for Mouse.

It is drafty. Food is scarce.

And now Fox has tracked her there.

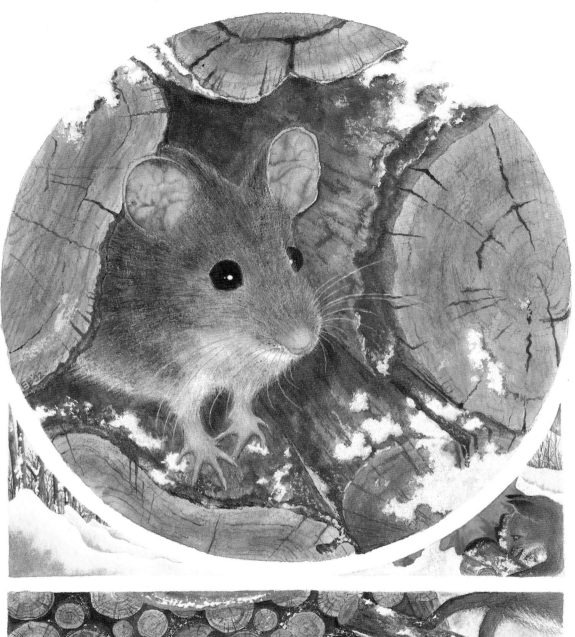

Look out, Mouse!

Tired as she is and hungry as she may be,
Fox is hungry too.

Quick now!

Under the snow crust, around the garden elf, along the split-rail fence.

Run, Mouse, run!

Phew! Clever Mouse.

She shivers. How thin the walls are —
thinner still, it seems, with Fox scratching
and yipping on the other side. What place
is this?

A shed piled high with discarded things,
broken things and boxes. Somewhere in
here Mouse must make a nest. Soon.

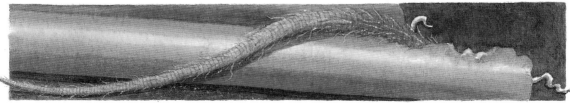

Her nose tells her where there might be food. But this box is already taken.

"Scat!" says the rat.

"No room in here," say the wood roaches.

Another box has become a moth hotel.
How they flutter at her.

Every level of the boxed city is alive with
busy creatures. Even her own kind will not
take Mouse in. There is nowhere for her.
Up she climbs. Weary, weary.

Finally there seems to be nothing left but boxes of books. Books are okay — the paper makes a nice soft nest — but what a lot of work it is to get through one! There just isn't time. So, as tired as she is, Mouse keeps climbing until there is only one box left.

What a find! Food: fruit and grain.

And in the box, what's this? A little house.

And something else — a roll of soft, warm felt.

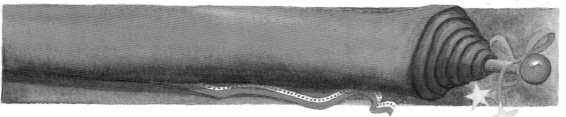

Mouse snacks a bit. The food revives her. She must get to work, but first just one more berry. There. Now she can start. Chew, chew, chew the soft felt. Place it just so. Her baby will not be long now.

At last he is born. Some of the others look in on her, on him. A curious spider, a mouse or two. Three sow bugs.

Mouse and Little Mouse stay there in the little house in the box at the top of the shed feeding on popcorn and cranberries. Little Mouse even finds one sugared almond. He shares it with his mother.

They live on next to nothing. But food is still running low. And where will they go now?

What's this?

Too late to run. Hide, Mouse!
Little Mouse, be quiet!

What a bumpy ride!

And then suddenly — warmth.
Fire burning safely in its own place.

What a wonderful home! What wonderful smells! But there are giants too, and
frightening noises. Mouse and Little
Mouse run from their home and hide
in a corner.

The children unroll the soft red felt.
An Advent calendar full of holes! "None
of the days are missing," says the middle
child. "Imagine that!" says the eldest.

Then the children carefully unwrap the
figures in the box. Wise men, Virgin,
husband, and baby; a boy with his lamb.
Then, carefully, carefully, the little house
itself: a creche, of course. "What a mess!"
says the eldest. "No," says the middle
one, "a nest."

The children look at the creche again in amazement. "You're both wrong," says the little one. "It's a *miracle.*"

So they place the baby child in the red felt nest, and gather the others around him so they can see the miracle for themselves.

And later that night, by the light of the fire, in the comforting glow, Mouse and Little Mouse can't help but agree.
A miracle indeed.

*For Laurie Lewis, who knows a lot about Christmas
and a lot about mice! — T. W.-J.*

*For my Mom and Dad, Bob, Barry, Valerie, Darl and Peter.
Together we have danced in and about the Miracle. — E. B.*

VIKING
Published by the Penguin Group
Penguin Books Canada Ltd, 10 Alcorn Avenue, Toronto, Ontario, Canada M4V 3B2
Penguin Books Ltd, 27 Wrights Lane, London W8 5TZ, England
Viking Penguin, a division of Penguin Books USA Inc., 375 Hudson Street,
New York, New York 10014, U.S.A.
Penguin Books Australia Ltd, Ringwood, Victoria, Australia
Penguin Books (NZ) Ltd, 182-190 Wairau Road, Auckland 10, New Zealand

Penguin Books Ltd, Registered Offices: Harmondsworth, Middlesex, England

First published 1993

10 9 8 7 6 5 4 3 2 1

Text copyright © Tim Wynne-Jones, 1993
Illustrations copyright © Elaine Blier, 1993

*Publisher's note: This book is a work of fiction. Names, characters, places and incidents
either are the product of the author's imagination or are used fictitiously, and any
resemblance to actual persons living or dead, events, or locales is entirely coincidental.*

Printed and bound in Italy on acid free paper ∞

Canadian Cataloguing in Publication Data

Wynne-Jones, Tim
    Mouse in the manger

ISBN 0-670-85027-6

I. Blier, Elaine, 1957- . II. Title.

PS8595.Y44M68 1993   jC813'.54   C92-095742-0
PZ7.W94Mo 1993